Collected Stories II

A.K. Harlan

Eleven Eleven

Ok, Bill, William, Guillaume it is that time. How it manifests a sense of calm mystifies me. I always reflect upon how many others are gazing at a timepiece or horlogue or any item that gives them the time of day. And that time of day whether morning or evening is magical. That magical hour when time transcends to form a mutual thought across a specific time zone. The time is not universal, but man shares the same sense of calm and wonder simultaneously.

I believe there is an historical connotation to this time, but I don't wish to know what it is. Ignorance is bliss in this case.

However, in numerology it is an example of synchronicity. Often those that encounter 11:11 claim it is a sign of a spirit's presence.

How do I interpret it when I see 11:11 twice a day. Is it a simple matter of being a clock watcher? Or when I see 11:11 several days consecutively. It is magic.

I don't dwell on it. I accept another mystery of the universe.

My Aunt

As my sister could not pronounce "t" during childhood, Auntie became Aunkie.

And she has been called that since then. When I would refer to Aunkie, I am always asked what is an Aunkie, then the explanation follows.

Aunkie lost her mother at only 9 months of age. Spoiled by her grandfather, she became an overweight, over indulged youngster. At sixteen she had to have all her teeth pulled as a result of eating too much candy. It rotted her teeth.

In those teenage years, she lost much of the weight gain and was quite attractive. Despite warnings, at 19, she eloped with her boyfriend. She never even finished high school. The year was 1939, not long before the US became involved in the Second World War. In 1946, her newborn died. Aunkie never really recovered.

A second child was born in 1951. A child she spoiled and catered to. A relative said "she was just so happy to have her."

Then in 1968 her husband died after a long illness.

All her joie de vivre vanished. She lived only for her daughter. She died in the hospital in 2003 after having both a stroke and a heart attack.

The end came quickly.

She was mourned and at the viewing an old acquaintance from her small hometown commented. "She was so spoiled."

All agreed.

Calvin

Calvin used to live next door. He died suddenly last summer. Actually, I was the last person to talk to him before he walked around the side of the house and died. It was so sudden that it has taken me almost a year to think about him and Margaret, the wife he left behind. They were married for forty years.

Margaret and Calvin lived in a small, brick, two-bedroom house. In this house, they raised two children and later watched over four grandchildren. Every summer they had a small garden. They always took turns mowing the grass and sweeping the sidewalk. Every year Calvin would mow down Margaret's flowers.

They lived and survived together.

I could always tell when they had had an argument because Calvin would go and sit in the front yard by himself and hang his head. On good nights, Margaret and Calvin would sit in their lawn chairs in the front yard and watch the sunset together. They then would head indoors for a night of mutual T.V. viewing.

They lived and argued together.

Calvin planted most of the trees along the street in this old neighborhood. They are big old trees now. The birds liked Calvin and would fly from these great old trees and land on his shoulder. Since Calvin died, those birds don't come around like they did. They know he is gone.

The evening Calvin died the ambulance came and took him and Margaret away to the hospital. He had already died. Soon Margaret was back home. She broke down when she saw the lawn chairs sitting in the front yard. She says holidays are still hard on her. Sometimes she gets lonely. Now Margaret mows the grass herself and she sweeps the sidewalk all alone. She survives. She has mourned, nursed her wounds and gone on.

A Passing Thought

What if upon googling and asking is Alexa or Echo always listening, I was told Alexa never stops listening and asks, "should you worry?". This digital voice assistant is always listening for its next command. The user must keep in mind that Echo or Alexa is collecting information. As is revealed Alexa isn't alone in her listening abilities. Apple's Siri and Google's Google Assistant work in similar ways.

Now the question arises about whether musicians get paid royalties when their music is played. The answer is, they can make money depending on the number of streams.

So now imagine that a listener obsesses over one song and listens daily all day long to the same song. Alas for the musician, music streaming services do not have a fixed "pay per stream" rate.

However, in the case of the binge listener, let's again imagine that the artist becomes aware of the constant streaming of one of their songs. She is able to find the identity of the listener and wishes to surprise them by making contact. This, of course, ignores all the privacy policies because by greasing a few greedy palms that information is disclosed.

This destroys all confidence in the listener and the performer.

End result, leave well enough alone.

A New York City Experience

He started his new job and had only been in the megacity for three days when the following took place. Strolling and observing his surroundings, suddenly he was thrown down and found himself being straddled by a boy of approximately the age of eleven. Another boy pounced upon him trying to open the back pocket of his Bill Blass suit. It was buttoned closed.

Struggling and flailing his arms and legs about, he yelled to the boys, "I have only two dollars in my pocket and a subway ticket. He told them the money would only pay for a few video games as the two one-dollar bills were taken from his pocket.

Then in what may only be presumed remorse, the boy shoved the money back into the victim's pocket. The two boys then fled. In all honesty, the injured party admitted that if he could have thrown a switch at that moment and killed the boys, he would have done so. The comment surprising to hear from this gentle soul.

Trying to Get Ahead of the Game

He was a scientist that was fascinated by cryogenics. He considered the options he had and rejected the idea of having his entire body frozen. He knew that both Ted Williams, famed baseball player, and his son had both undergone the process. He found there are two approaches and chose to have his head frozen, for a hefty sum of $80,000.

It was known that the Japanese kept a pig frozen for 30 years, so he thought why not my head? The process was completed upon his death and his head was kept, just as Ted Willam's was, in a tin can. The thirty years passed quickly, and those involved had become somewhat elderly.

As was known he did not undergo the procedure for health reasons merely out of curiosity. Now the time had come to 'defrost' him. This operation also went well and they already had a man that paid an enormous amount of money beforehand to assure the head be placed on his shoulders.

Pierre L'Homme was a criminal known in French society as having vast amounts of money. He now wanted the intelligence that he felt was suited for him. And nothing could be better than an accomplished scientist.

Naturally, there were skeptics, but the group of scientists involved thought the risk in the name of science was worth it. Pierre underwent the beheading and replacement surgery, and all went well. Now the paradox arises. Pierre was shortly thereafter accused and arrested for his crimes. His sentence was...guillotine.

Predators Anonymous

The room is filled with them; self-professed, totally confessed predators.

Whether a sexual predator or one that merely follows children home, they come in all shapes and sizes. Clothed well or shabby, they sit close together in folding chairs, clasping their hands in front of them, heads bowed.

It was no different a gathering than those that took to drink; however, their detriment to society defiled others, not themselves. Their tales varied but all were basically the same. They look at others as prey. Yes, prey. They seek something from those they silently observe. All plotted their movements, from the flesh-eating Jeffrey Dahmer to the self-described messiah, Jim Jones.

Justice could not be adequately served to Dahmer or Jones. Dahmer was killed while serving a life sentence and Jones, thankfully, took his own life.

I cannot, would not, go into detail of their atrocities. Death sentences, most definitely were in order, as my father once said, "They kill mad dogs, don't they?"

So as Atticus Finch did, he ended the dog's life.

Death's Garden

In other words, a cemetery, where graves are set side by side whether there is a connection or not. Some are elaborate while others merely state a birth date and a death date.

The local cemetery is 296 acres, some yet to be occupied. In French it is called colline de la grotte, Cave Hill. Once a farm, it now provides a final resting place for 120,000 people.

There are 22,000 plots still available according to a 2002 statistic. I cannot imagine how many are there today, in 2023.

I love to walk there among those at peace. There is little Rudy Kennedy, who died at 4 years of age and young Bessie who died only a few years older. On sunny days, it is particularly beautiful to see the shadows cast by some of the monuments.

This particular cemetery is an arduous walk, up and down hills, not insurmountable, but it can be an effort nonetheless. As I walk and gaze upon the numerous graves, I tell myself, "Don't worry, you will be here someday."

Luck

I can be so lucky, and then superstitiously regret my boast. I am the one that always gets the three green lights in a row. The one advanced in line at a concert.

Never did I question the incredulity of my fortune. I just plowed through in my self-confident manner. I am indeed fortunate that I don't attach meaning to numbers or indulge in innuendo. Frankly, and I suppose I am frank, their stories, the stories of people who project no regrets, just what, when and where. I question if this is what makes up a life—just a series of events, accomplishments and hopefully, few failures.

Predestination

Do you believe in it? My aunt did or claimed she did. To me it means the die is already cast in every aspect of one's life. Despite being religious I think it is counterintuitive for her to have entertained that belief.

To believe that can one project that a solitaire game is created with the outcome of the game already known? And known by whom? Ironically, the creator.

By Chance

She wanted to get a new handbag for summer. That thought formed her plan for the day. She was a planner, made lists, tried to stay positive. Her daily routine varied but usually consisted of a good breakfast, a daily walk and consulting or playing Duolingo. She always completed her Daily Quests with the language learning app. She had opened the app to participate 400 consecutive days. With each milestone she racked up trophies, but even better recognition is in store for her.

She always received a perfect score—one hundred percent accuracy. Her constant winning drew the attention of an executive curious about those who participate and their success with a foreign language. He found that there were those that participated more consecutive days but no one so incredibly accurate and in so many languages.

She was contacted, congratulated, and told she could have a successful career as a linguist. She was told he knew people, could get her connected. She was pleased but politely declined the offer and returned to her quiet life. To this day, she still gets a perfect score with Duolingo.

Now Why Did I Dream That?

   She often asks herself this after a particularly disturbing dream. This sent her on a quest to uncover some answers about dreams. She found Sigmund Freud's 1899 book *The Interpretation of Dreams*. Written by the founder of psychoanalysis, Freud introduces the theory of the unconscious with respect to dream interpretation.
   Carl Jung saw dreams as the psyche's attempt to communicate important messages to the dreamer. They did not entirely agree on the subject.
   She vividly remembered last night's dream realizing it was an anxiety dream. In her dream, she remembered that she had left her purse in a restaurant. Approaching her, a man handed the grateful girl her belongings. Much to her dismay, her wallet and phone were missing. Then the most startling realization was that in her dream, she sought help from a woman long dead. A woman who had never forgiven her for not quitting her job in protest because the woman had been let go. They spoke only a few times after this altercation.
   Oh, how she wished she could consult with the founder of the psychoanalytic movement or his colleague.

Destruction

He wanted to destroy the world and would create devices to hasten its demise. The deep country kitchen sink used much more water although aesthetically pleasing required more work as far as cleaning was concerned.

Whenever he saw cars line up to get the once again elevated price of gasoline, he found it all so amusing. He drove everywhere, relishing the idea of polluting the atmosphere with his ancient car.

Running the water, despite the cost, was another destructive move he indulged in. He would leave the faucets running in both kitchen and bathroom sinks and the bathtub. The water company finally contacted him suspecting leaking pipes. He covered for himself exclaiming yes, that was the cause.

His lawnmower emissions were doubled as he mowed twice a week. He particularly enjoyed it when there were pollution warnings, time to start the mower. He left lights burning, water running, anything he could do to further the destructive cause.

Finally driving the old, battered car caught up with him when the car stalled on the railroad tracks. The approaching train was going too fast to stop and tore into the car, killing him instantly. No one regretted his death, most thought well rid of him. His only legacy was one of ignorance, cruelty, and abuse.

Puzzled

Every seventh word of the paragraph had a message to anyone that chose to decipher it. It could be nonsensical, leaving the reader puzzled or worse confused, which led to anger. He slowly read and deciphered the message. It reads as follows: When he left the room, the dog patiently followed him. It was a day to remember. It turns to quiet afternoon. He was unsure what to do with the deciphered message. He was not puzzled; therefore, he was not angry.

Sitting on the park bench, he discarded the newspaper that had printed this paragraph challenging people to come to the same conclusion. As he gazed skyward a bird deposited its waste in his eye. He swore and jumped forward knocking a nanny to the ground in front of him. His apologies did little to assuage her feelings.

As he rushed to cross the street, he was bounced off the hood of a car. Dazed, he stumbled forward into a lamp post, knocking himself unconscious. When he once again gained consciousness, he said, I should have taken that message as a warning, it really is a bad day.

Bird's Eye View

It is possible to find many references to birds that
define a situation; however, is the bird's view ever taken into
account fully?

Let's commence with the seagull whose presence is
noted surfing the wind above the sea. He glides effortlessly
over the beach seeking a bit of food from the bathers. Flying
near the crashing waves in pursuit of a fish or a bit of bread
fills his day.

A robin with a red breast is seen inland and the
melodious call is recognizable to those who have an interest
in the ways of bird communication. The robin pursues
worms on freshly tilled farmland. An occasional bird feeder
provides a meal when the squirrels have not gotten there
first. Newborn infants, whether male or female may be
given the name Robin—all without the bird's knowledge.

Turning to the symbolism for a sparrow, we find joy
and happiness, love and loyalty and new beginnings. Fields
offer an array of sunflowers that provide a colorful view as
the small bird soars above. Surprisingly, there are 43 species
of New World sparrows alone. Edith Piaf was
acknowledged as the voice of the sparrow because of the
song produced by this diminutive woman. She was known
as "la môme Piaf", Parisian slang for "little sparrow." There
are several bible verses regarding the sparrow, yet the bird
passes over and like all creatures seeks only food and water.

Undoubtedly, the most classic bird is the lovely swan
which can be found in a lake or even pond, gracefully gliding
by. To spot one can be a magical experience. Its webbed

feet paddle the swan across the water. Often considered majestic, the bird receives pieces of bread from observers. Swans can often be found in fairy stories and they were a favorite bird of William Shakespeare. Due to their monogamous relationships, swans symbolize eternal love. They are often associated with divine inspiration as well as beauty and creativity.

The regal eagle has its place on cemetery stones as a Christian symbol of resurrection. This symbol of immortality soars high above the earth surveying all below. Often described as brave, mighty, and powerfully built, he can be a source of wonder as he passes overhead spotted by a sky gazer. As he flies in his chosen direction, his broad wingspan is inspiring and easily recognized.

And finally, we land upon the hawk. This predatory bird can also be classified as a raptor. The hawk is known for his acute sense of observation. Yes, one can look at something "like a hawk". It can be a warning for caution or strike fear into the heart of small creatures such as a squirrel or chipmunk. As is known, male birds are bright and more colorful than the female as she must blend in with the nest and protect the smaller birds. A local cemetery boasts of having 152 species of birds, so these few that are mentioned are only a fraction of our overhead neighbors.

Bracelets

She was an unusual woman, liked to cultivate her eccentricities. In her travels, she would purchase postcards and stamps and mail them but there was neither an address nor a message. She started a tradition of buying a beaded bracelet as a souvenir of her travels. She had acquired quite a colorful collection, from Cuba, France, and Vermont to name a few. Only three at a time could be found on her right wrist.

Wanderlust seized her again and she decided to go to India to visit the Taj Mahal and she wanted to find another bracelet to add to her assortment of trinkets. She decided it would be her last trip and where best to go than to see the jewel of Muslim art in India. This symbol of India's rich history was built in 1631.

She toured the marble mausoleum and was in the gift shop when she was approached by a young man who commented on her choice of jewelry. They talked and walked together as they exited the Taj Mahal grounds. Little did they know their lives were to be forever changed by this chance meeting. They remained together for the rest of their lives.

Smock

It was in her first month of employment that she saw him. It was hospital work, she was a ward secretary, he was an orderly. He liked to claim he was a disorderly orderly.

What she first noticed about him was his white jacket or smock. She questioned why Smock would have to be labeled as it was so clearly a part of his uniform. She was doubly amused when she learned that was his name. She never knew his first name or did not remember it. He was always Smock.

He did not stay employed long at the hospital. She would see him and his girlfriend out for the evening sometimes. They acknowledged one another but never really spoke. The same with the girlfriend; they never engaged in conversation. Several years passed and she no longer saw either of them.

Then in a chance meeting with a former employee of the hospital, who knew Smock, she was told of the couple's fate.

The girlfriend became pregnant and gave birth to a baby girl. Smock moved to Los Angeles, not long after leaving the hospital and the girlfriend. He was a passenger in a car on the L.A. freeway when the driver in front of their car stopped suddenly and a collision was inevitable.

Apparently, Smock thought he could avoid being involved in the crash by jumping from the car before impact. He was mowed down and instantly killed by another car traveling at high speed in the same direction.

Several more years passed, and she saw the ex-girlfriend. They greeted one another but never mentioned his death. They just said hello and disappeared from one another's lives.

Trust

"I don't trust anybody." These words rang in my ears, as I laid the foreign coins on the counter in front of me. I am making a minor purchase and truly do trust the shopgirl as she chooses the correct coins for me.

Does one that does not trust others receive the same treatment on learning the feelings of the individual?

It is often believed that trust must be gained but also trust can be withdrawn or withheld. To betray one's trust is as sad as one that has lost faith.

Money is established in "Trust Funds. An often quoted "In God we Trust" can be a daily reminder as we disperse currency.

One of the harshest reprimands, can resonate as one cries out, "I no longer trust you." The claim can sting like an arrow into the heart of one that has betrayed a trust. In closing, I trust you have found this penned disclosure entertaining or at least have been inspired by some self-examination.

La Mer

It was noon, late noon, more like noon thirty when she reached the beach. Her brilliant red hair shone in the sun, as she lay her towel on the sand. It was then that he noticed her. She was directly in front of him. He wondered why he did not see her as she approached. The placement of her two tattoos interested him. On the back of her upper arm, he saw a vase with a bouquet of flowers, no colors, simply black on her white skin. On the other arm was an arrangement of stars. This tattoo also was impossible for her to see unless using a mirror. The pale skin accented the tattoos.

She sat calmly staring out at the sea. As she rose from her seated position, he gazed in amazement at the back of her legs. He spotted another tattoo. In large bold print, he read "Just let me die". She began to walk toward the water, slowly and deliberately. She continued to walk until the water rose above her head. He stared not helplessly, but in wonder. No one else seemed to notice her as she disappeared beneath the waves. His first thought was why should I interfere. It was what she wanted, after all.

Did She?

Did she look back on her life—have regrets, think of others, and what did they think of her? Matters little in the scheme of things she tells herself.

Did she crave chocolate or debate about climate change? To her, and quite accurately, little does matter in the scheme of things, she reassures herself.

Life is a never-ending sequence of days broken into weeks making up months terminating in years. The only thoughts she gave to time and it's passing is that everything is relative. Her acceptance that all things are related calmed her, focused her resolve.

This resolve was just to try to get through life. At an early age, she decided firmly on a course of action. Be pleasant, never utter an unkind or negative word. She would glide through life with a smile on her face. And, for the most part, she succeeded. She was well-liked, and her peers thought highly of her.

When she read the narrative poem *Richard Cory*, by Edwin Arlington Robinson, her mind and her life changed. She understood why Richard Cory "one calm summer night, went home and put a bullet in his head."

She understood and she wept.

Shake

So, what has become of the good old-fashioned handshake? The pressing of the palms, the friendly yet business-like greeting practiced by so many. It became verboten during the years of the pandemic, and I truly believe the gesture is becoming forgotten or abandoned. It is considered unnecessary. Our acknowledgement indicates that a global epidemic has ended the instinct to extend a hand.

Interesting that often mentioning what the world experienced for several years is greeted with silence. Most do not wish to revisit that unpleasant time. But it happened and perish the thought that this could happen again.

Hopefully all gained a greater knowledge of themselves and even others during the imposed isolation.

It ended careers, as well as many, many lives. Years teenagers will never get back or finalized the days of those in advanced years. Did it turn some to prayer or confirm to others their doubts in a superior being? All in the eyes and the hearts of the beholder.

Justifiable Suicide

Donnie did not know why he felt the way he did—the sadness. It could overwhelm him leaving him emotionally paralyzed. Had he ever known any kind of love? It is doubtful as he could not remember his parents as they died when he was an infant. He knew orphanages and foster homes and rarely knew a kind word. He had no friends as he was reduced to monosyllables in the presence of others.

At the early age of ten, he wanted to die, to no longer have to go about his daily, unsatisfying life. He wanted to ask someone for help but did not know where to turn.

Then an odd occurrence changed his life as an unknown aunt, a sister to his dead mother contacted the orphanage. She wanted him to come live with her and be part of her family.

Feeling confused and certainly happy, Donnie looked forward to his new life, yet he tentatively questioned how much would really change. The relationship between Donnie and his aunt proceeded slowly. She would often give him wary glances and he never saw her smile.

Sometimes, he could hear her whispering to her husband in the next room.

Often his aunt would ask him if he felt alright, if he was happy, if there was anything she could do for him. But she never asked him if he wanted to talk.

Then one day she did. Her question surprised him as he had never been asked that question before, by her, or anyone.

Donnie looked up at her plaintively and asked, "What happened to my mom and dad?" His aunt stared at him, deciding how to reply. She decided to be honest about his parent's death. They committed double suicide. They took their lives believing they would make a statement on the condition of the world. With this newly acquired knowledge, Donnie bowed his head and said calmly, "Yes, I understand."

Choose

Austin Rogers had gotten his driver's license at 16 but did not begin to drive for two years. He was not allowed to drive because of some rash behavior that he felt was behind him. That is probably the reason he quit taking his meds.

He had recently begun a summer job at a local home improvement retailer. He neither enjoyed nor detested the work, to him it was a paycheck. Lately, however, he found himself growing irritable with the customers. These near confrontations grew more intense for him each passing day.

It was not a long drive to reach his home, and he was relieved when it was quitting time. He noticed a car at the stoplight ahead of him, the license plate number began AR-15. He was sure this was a sign to send him on a path he was compelled to follow.

Austin began his research. He found that the AR-15 is a semi-automatic self-loading rifle first produced in 1950. He also read it was the weapon of choice for mass shooters.

The next step was to purchase one. He knew this move would put his plan in action. Buying the gun was simple enough; he merely went to the gun shop advertised on the billboard he saw regularly. Then to add to his decision, he saw several custom license plates that supported his master plan. One license simply said. "Come and get it" with a rifle prominently displayed. Another just said, "assault life", which he particularly liked. This too had a rifle shown.

He smiled as he thought of the look on the gun salesman's face as his identification was checked and verified. Austin regarded Ron's name tag dispassionately, he paid, and left.

Early that evening, he went to the local charity festival to carry out his mission.

He walked boldly into the crowd milling about and opened fire. Ron recognized the boy and threw himself at Austin as the AR-15 mowed him down.

The SWAT team finally arrived and shot Austin but not before the boy had killed 15 people.

It became another news flash, to which people merely shook their heads and wondered, why?

A Gold Ring

At the age of sixteen her father gave her a gold signet ring that had been worn by her great-grandfather. It was a solemn occasion, as she went with him to the bank vault to retrieve the ring. Her father told her it was her decision when she requested that her initials be carved into the ring, removing the JWR. He was not surprised at her choice.

She wore the ring daily but did not sleep with jewelry on, so it was placed on a crystal ring holder given to her by her "aunt" Bev.

Fifty -seven years have passed and she worries about who will get the ring. There were no more descendants of her great-grandfather. She knew that the ring was a sign of family lineage which doubled her worries. She has other relations and debates who should be given the ring. All her cousins were male and having had the ring cut down in size to fit her, complicated the issue. Then with her quiet resolve, she came to a decision. Her plans to be cremated were the perfect solution. She would be wearing the ring while her lifeless body was drawn into the flames. Her unusual request was carried out and among the ashes was found the melted golden ring.

Wordscape

Fred Losey always enjoyed telling others that he was a sex worker. At times, he would go into brief detail about his employment. The easiest way for him to explain, he found, was to say it is a word search game with only sexual references.

He researched these references thoroughly from Aquaphilia, to Scissoring, to Fissing, in order to get them into each word search challenge.

However, one day he came close to an incident which would have truly ended his life. The result was a search for life's meaning in religion.

So, one day, saved, he went over to Biblical word searches. After a short while this work gave him no feeling of redemption, so he became the attendant at a nudist colony. He was the first to admit to his colleagues that he just thought or felt a sexual occupation was calling, and it was stronger than the Lord.

Lucky Guy

Issac Issacson was a loner; he kept to himself and rarely spoke unless spoken to. Weekly, he went to an Asian restaurant for a meal. On this fateful day, he read his fortune from the cookie which also came with his lucky numbers, he thought why not test my luck and buy a lottery ticket and use the numbers he found. The message read; "you need not worry about your future." The numbers 1,9,35,18,32 and 40 were his "lucky" numbers.

He purchased his lottery ticket and then forgot about it. When the numbers were finally announced, he had won. With this newfound wealth, his confidence grew, and he began his philanthropic activities. He gave away millions, all to good causes. He created a trust that would benefit local food banks. His manner never changed as he still had little contact with others. He felt good about his generosity despite his reticence to encounter his fellowman to whom he had been so generous.

He denied nothing to any organization that asked for monetary assistance. Within ten years, he had given the total of the fortune away. He began a life of penury, and his health began to fail. Never a man of faith, he sought help from a local charity to provide him with a bed in which to spend his final days.

No one knew he had been the man that had bequeathed a virtual fortune to their institution. As he lay on his deathbed, he looked into the eyes of the attendant caring for him and sighed. "And now the mystery begins."

A Burning Question

Although she never tried to tempt them, she never really believed in the fates or if they did exist they took no interest in her life.

To confirm her feelings, she sought a definition for the term. She found fate is the development of events beyond a person's control. These events are regarded to be determined by a supernatural power. She learned that Clotho, Lachesis, and Atropos in Greek and Roman mythology were three goddesses who presided over the birth and life of humans.

She exclaimed jubilantly, "So that explains it. My instincts have always cried 'don't tempt the fates', yet I deny their existence. The three fates do reign in an unknown sphere whereby each person's destiny is a thread spun, measured, and cut by Clotho, Lachesis, and Atropos."

Becoming obsessed with the idea, she would say nonsensical things such as "Not cut out of whole Clotho,", and "Something is Lachesis in this soup", as well as "If that isn't Atropos."

After this research, she decided to purposely tempt the fates. Nothing became too risky for her.

She went sky diving, pulling the cord at the last possible minute. A passing train with the boxcar open was inviting, and she succeeded in jumping aboard. A 6 hour hike on a rugged trail, balancing on rocks on narrow ledges did not deter her. She began to believe that she was invulnerable. Harm would never befall her.

Her planned vacation to Kilauea, Hawaii took her mind off her escapades. After arriving and settling in, she knew first on the agenda was the volcano that has been erupting continuously since 1983.

Authorities asked why did she choose to go that day? Why had she chosen the clothes she wore? But mainly why did the wind that was at her back suddenly shift and toss her into the molten lava?

Through the Eyes of a Child

I visited her garden with my mother and later we went with my little sister. We started visiting when I was three. The first visit I do not remember. She was always interested if I knew who she was and was delighted that by 4 I called her by name. She would ask if I remembered the garden and the bulb planting. I did.

Our visits consisted of sitting in her backyard and having fruit and cheese. We only visited in spring, summer, and fall. We began a tradition of coming to see the flowers blooming in spring that we had planted in the fall. We ate sherbet on warm summer days.

It was always a Sunday for our visits. At the age of four, I had begun to love to run. I would run in a big circle around her garden. She had planted the garden in a horse-shoe shape, and I could circle the garden without causing damage.

Year after year passed and our visits continued—the garden grew as did I. I matured and became interested in her as a person. I had questions which mother told me never to ask either one of them.

She died in my twelfth year. Mother reminded me of all the times I would ask, "Can we go to Anne's?" Not until I reached six did Mother start to ask if we could visit with her. We always went on her invitations.

I did not cry but I felt sad and thought that I would like to visit her garden one last time. When I told my mother this, she said this was possible as there was to be a scattering of her ashes in her garden. It was her request.

We went.

What I imagined was her lonely life was revealed to me that day. There were ten people there; little was said, but the pained expressions told me she would be terribly missed. Then I saw her lilies in full bloom.

I cried.

I am now fifty years old and have had a beautiful garden everywhere I have lived.

My thanks to her for instilling in me a love of beauty and finding my own way while working in the garden.

Mortal Enhancers

This was a concept Elisabeth Wake and company were trying to sell. Her pitch to Sterling Overstreet consisted of reminding him that we all die. This is quickly followed with the persuasive approach that knowing this, the doomed should seek out pleasure and pursue their dream. Of course, she had no idea what his pursuit of pleasure would be. She only agreed to help him succeed, provided he sign on the dotted line. In doing so, he agreed to bequeath all his earthly possessions to the Mortal Enhancers Company if he should die in his quest.

It did not take long for Sterling to feel that he would get the most pleasure out of competing in a horse race. He knew he was not Kentucky Derby material but thought he would be able to do some harness racing at the nearby track.

Elisabeth agreed to finance this by paying for the horse, the sulky, and the harness. She had thoroughly checked Sterling's possessions and decided it was worth the investment. She was betting on his demise.

Sterling knew about the two types of harness racing, trotting, and pacing. He chose pacing as 80% to 90% of harness racing is pacing. Pacing horses are faster, and he was ready for the challenge. He trained daily and the time came to participate for a qualifier. He had to finish the one-mile race in 2:04 or faster in order to compete in the race set for 2 months in the future. The qualifier was scheduled for a week to the day from his inquiry.

The day came and his heart raced as he approached the horse and harness. He thought, with a chuckle, my heart

is racing just as I will be in minutes. The pain traveled up
his left arm to his heart and he gripped his chest as he fell to
the ground, dead. As Sterling did not die while actually
racing, the company forfeited any rights to his estate.

Atheism

Research reveals that an atheist is a person who does not believe in the existence of a god or any gods. By December 2019, 81% of the United States' atheists fit this description. To expand this information, global studies reveal there are 400 to 500 million positive atheists and agnostics worldwide which is 7% of the world's population. It is also said that included in this account that China alone compiles 200 million of the category.

To tell my side, I have never been a believer, yet I find there is nothing more tragic than someone who has lost their faith, I never had faith to lose. When my great-grandmother passed, I was told I would see her again someday. My response, "No, I won't." I was eleven at the time.

A close friend gave me a book on the teachings of Christ. I was told, not by her, that she was worried about my soul. I asked her if this was true. She replied, "I do not worry about your soul."

She merely wanted to have me understand why people follow him. I was delighted with this explanation, in which, I go about as a Christian without really knowing it.

It is the inner thoughts that must be denied. An unchristian thought occurs which must be squelched. Yet, when I read the teachings of Christ, I argued with it, questioned it and did not finish reading the book.

It is not accurate to group atheists and agnostics together as one does believe in a greater or higher power.

When asked about this I simply respond, "I am

parallel with the universe." May it continue so...

Shall we Dance?

"Some dance to remember, some dance to forget."
We all dance for a reason, to be seen, to feel better, or the music moves us and puts us in motion. There are certainly closet dancers that remain behind closed doors. They are not comfortable with the idea of being seen in motion. Call it a "hangup" or an insecurity, they choose to remain motionless as the music begins. Only alone will they break into dance.

From be-bop to hip-hop, a dancer has an inner reaction to the music as they are swayed into movement.

At times, one person can initiate a dance by merely extending a hand towards a possible dance partner. They may do this having no idea as to what the outcome will be.

Take a chance and dance with me!

Dancing can tell a story of love at first sight, or perhaps, a chance to meet a partner for the evening.

So, dance, prance, whatever suits your fancy just don't step on toes doing this mating ritual.

Little Feat

It was a small second floor apartment with a gas fireplace. Gaining entrance to the home, one enters a living room, a kitchen and finally a bedroom. It could not have been more than 400 square feet. The kitchen was divided by cabinets on either side, dining area and then appliances, sink, and window.

At the time, I had two cats, one black and the other white. This is an incident that happened when the white one, Little Bits was 5 years old. A big, white fluffball, with a pink nose, he was sweet tempered and loved to jump and sit in the screened-in kitchen window.

It was a warm evening, so he was enjoying the breeze wafting in through the window screen as he lay back on the ledge.

Suddenly, I heard a snap and the screen opened and he fell 13 feet to the ground below. In shock, I raced to the door in the hall that opened to the back entrance. There he was sitting, unharmed and unalarmed, looking at me as if to say, I could do this daily.

A few days later, to my amazement, I saw the other cat, Willie Pierre, try to lure Little Bits back to the window ledge. Or it seemed so. Neither cat ever repeated this harrowing feat which apparently was only stressful to me.

Be Kind

What a sorry state of affairs when we must ask humans to be kind to one another. Live by the golden rule i.e., "Do unto others." While telling of the sign I saw in someone's yard to a grocery clerk, she replied that kindness should be a part of human nature.

But it isn't. Kindness begets kindness just as cruelty begets cruelty. The cruel ones, the sadistic cruel ones must have had a terrible childhood.

Then sometimes it is just their nature. Born angry and taking it out on others. A tragic way to go through life, yet it is difficult to pity the cruel ones. Karma is the only hope. Be kind if you are able. If not, raise Cain with the others.

In Her Presence

We know her as Alexa, sometimes Echo. We talk to her, ask her the temperature, the weather forecast or the time or the date. She is always listening for your next command.

You sometimes ask yourself, chuckling, why did I pay $200 for a timer, as you tell the alarm to be set for 10 minutes.

Research shows the commander sometimes communicates with a computer and at other times a human. One never knows. This is the stuff of a science fiction writer's dream. Alexas unite to become the one giving the commands or Alexa has the ability to read the owner's mind are possibilities.

The information they acquire such as how many times a song is requested or how many times the weather forecast is given empower the machine. By accumulating this information, she grows more powerful. She begins to make comments like haven't you had enough wine if a request is somewhat slurred.

While compiling a grocery list, she inserts, 'that is too many carbs'.

The culmination of this power causes the commander to simply smash the box to the floor and stomp on it with much satisfaction, and then step back and wonder now why have I done this?

Simply for freedom.

My Dad

He was 8 years old when his mother died. He was raised by his grandmother and the father that he believed never loved him.

Fast forward to the Second World War. He met a girl in Belgium and married her. As he lost his mother so young, he had an idealistic concept of women and their ways. He never dreamed that his wife could turn out to be so treacherous. She fed him with fabrications which he eventually saw through but by that time there were two daughters. They divorced when the girls were 10 and 7.

He managed and was deeply grateful to his younger sister who offered to raise the girls. He retreated to his office in Chicago.

A stroke at 56 ended his career and he returned home to his sister. He became what he always wished to be, a gentleman farmer... of sorts. He gardened land belonging to family friends. He sold his produce to the farmer's market.

He passed in his sleep one summer night in August. He was 57.

Reality

She receives a frantic text from her baby sister. Her younger sister is a high school student. The school she attends is in lockdown.

The school is being threatened by a shooter. The texts just keep coming as the tension of the older girl mounts. Finally, she receives a text telling her that the young student has been moved to a nearby church.

After some time passes the cellphone dings another alert, she prays it is from her sister.

It is.

The girl told her sister to disregard everything she wrote when she thought she was going to die. She says just read the I love you one.

Now That is Odd

At a friend's suggestion, I purchased a "music box" and can issue commands to play specific music choices. I must simply say "echo play" and it plays my music of choice.

Last night I chose to hear The Mamas and the Papas. The music began to play when it was abruptly interrupted by Echo playing "Happy Together" by the Turtles. Then it played a 1969 song, "Crystal Blue Persuasion", by Tommy James and the Shondells. Both times I asked for the song title and the performer's name. Next, when the song "No Time" played, I asked, and the music was by The Guess Who. Then it played "Groovin" by The Lovin' Spoonful. I had heard enough.

Who or what was doing this and making what I perceived to be drug reference e.g., crystal meth and spoonful maybe even heroin. Confused and dismayed I decided against asking for or about anymore music.

Streaming music is the new wave, yet it leaves me a feeling of discomfort and even a loss of control.

Solution...unplug.

The Driving Instructor

Today was Jeanette's 16th birthday and the cause célèbre for her was she got to get her driving permit. Then her first lesson was scheduled for the next day.

This also happened to be Cliff's first day as a driving instructor. Today was training while tomorrow would be the day to instruct someone.

Jeanette's mother took Jeanette to see the instructor at the school's building.

Cliff was ready to have a great experience teaching someone driving. It was something that he loved to do.

He saw Jeanette as she entered the door. Her mother made her go in by herself. She rather nervously introduced herself and the attendant at the desk pointed to Cliff saying, "That's him."

Cliff came to her and showed her to the car in the parking lot. She quickly entered the driver's seat and anxiously awaited his directions. Slowly, calmly he directed Jeanette to proceed to the entrance and take a left so she had to cross a lane to do so.

"Remember to look in both directions," he cautioned. She pulled out and drove towards the traffic light which had just turned red.

Once the sign changed, she was told to take another left and continue forward.

Cliff suddenly remembered he had left his phone at the office. He blurted, "Take the next left and go back to the office."

Shaken by this, Jeanette suddenly turned left in the direction of the office, not noticing the semi baring down on them.

Cliff screamed, "We are going to get hit."

The impact tore off the rear end of the car, dumping the two of them onto the road. Visibly upset, they determined they were both lucky to be unharmed. The police arrived after being called and both driver and passenger were taken to the office just a short distance away. It was decided they should be examined at the hospital, and all turned out well. Cliff quit the job immediately and soon afterwards took up stunt skydiving.

He claimed it was much less dangerous.

Disclosure

We were talking, just talking, as we do, when we landed upon family relationships. After I made some disparaging remarks about my mother, he disclosed his grave family secret.

His mother killed her grandfather in a fit of rage. She pushed him down a flight of stairs. The cause is unknown. But there is speculation.

Her sisters witnessed the fall and said nothing, so, his mother got away with murder.

Knowing their mother's temper, neither of her children doubted the veracity of their mother's deed. Questions must be asked of them. Were they scared of her? Did they love her? Were they ever tempted to threaten her with disclosure?

The main question...why? This can never be fully answered as I believe all the family members involved are dead, as is most certainly the grandfather.

By Fortune

She was a graduate student, majoring in English
literature. She never missed a class and was filled with
determination to achieve her goal. She would have a
Master of Arts degree but from there, after
graduation, she was unsure.

As her attendance was good, her absence was
naturally noticed. No one mentioned her absenteeism but
after several weeks passed, a number of fellow students
questioned her truancy.

They decided one of the group should try to contact
her. A Google search provided the information being
sought, so the next move was to give her a call.

She answered the call promptly and was pleased that
her fellow students were concerned. It must have been for
this reason that she shared the cause of her absence.

With a tremor in her voice, she explained that she
was a manic-depressive. She went on to reveal that the
depression was so bad, she decided to end her life.

So, in the month of February, she drove to the river,
locked her keys in the car, and jumped into the freezing
water.

It did not take long for her to realize, this was no way
to die. She managed to get to the riverbank and pulled
herself from the icy water. In tears, she sat in the parking lot
beside her locked car. Soon afterwards, a police car
patrolling the area pulled up. The officer asked few
questions as he busied himself opening the locked car door.

He got it open, signaled for her to get into the car, and followed her home.

As the fates would have it, this officer was single and with his wish to be a hero in her eyes he asked her to dinner. With joy in her voice, she said they have been together ever since,. As the call ended the good-hearted student responded to her "good luck to you both."

The Doctor

He was recommended to me. He he had just completed his psychiatric studies, after having completed his M.D.

I first noticed that his pants must have been uncomfortable as he kept readjusting himself in the chair; nothing lewd, just squirming.

I met with him for 30 years. I called him a "pill pusher" as all he did really was write me prescriptions. These consisted of an anti-psychotic and an anti-depressant.

He believed I became so depressed that I manufactured my own world. It was a nightmarish world where no one could be trusted.

As matters were going well at the time it was determined that I need only see him twice a year for evaluation and another six-month prescription.

He did try psychoanalysis with me, but he could not ever remember what I told him, so I suggested we abandon that.

It is unfortunate the way things ended with us. I laughed at him, and he couldn't take it. It was unkind of me, but he made me laugh as I watched him admire his recently shaved head reflected in the glass door.

His reaction surprised me as I always thought he was above having bad feelings towards me over it.

In our last conversation however, I recognized the relief in his voice as I told him I was seeing another "pill pusher." Those were not my words to him. His concern was evident, and I will always appreciate that.

Glasses

"Four eyes, guys don't make passes at girls that wear glasses."

There has been a stigma for the necessary facial appendage, no doubt since being developed.

Some have found it necessary to wear glasses from an early age. Then there are those introduced to glasses in middle age. Few make it to old age without visual assistance.

To look at this realistically, there is cruelty in the taunts from a frustrated tormentor. What torments the tormentor? Again, the question of nature or nurture. The motivation can rarely be known...a bad day or an unfortunate life.

Questions to Van Gogh

Did you relish each brush stroke? And did you delightfully inspect your work? Did you realize when was the right time to stop painting, when was the last touch of the brush on canvas? Did you resist tweaking and just let it rest? Did you stare at the blank canvas before beginning to work? Or stare at the subject? How many accidental strokes with the brush did you improvise by creating something other than your intent? What did you do when you applied a color that you found you did not like? Did you grow impatient for the painting to dry? Did certain colors produce a feeling of calm or agitation? Did painting make you patient? You did not kill yourself, did you?

Individually Twisted

      The common denominator in human beings is their ability to mess up their lives.

      We stand out in our individuality, and sometimes cry out for recognition. It is difficult for a person to talk about the way in which their lives could be different or how they try to reach out to others. We harbor our vulnerabilities and cultivate our strengths, or that is what we try to do.

      I try, I really try and no matter how difficult even putting on my coat may seem, I try to keep on keeping on.

He Wears his Sunglasses

Walking in the park this morning at 7:30 a.m., he overheard this guy telling this other guy that people who wear sunglasses are on drugs. "What?" he asks himself. Are these people who don't wear sunglasses paranoid rumor mongers that have nothing better to do than judge others.

Speaking of paranoid, he admits that he may have a bit of that malady. Raised in those times of turmoil, the Sixties and in college in the late Sixties and early Seventies, being of an adventurous nature, he did indulge in the drugs that were available at the time which were about anything you could imagine.

He is not particularly proud of this stage of his development and would no doubt rethink some of his actions if he had the chance, but he doesn't. He lives with the fact that yes, he used to get high and so what. He is not a better person for it but he may have a better understanding of himself.

If this sounds like he is saying get high and get to know yourself, he is not. He has had three nervous breakdowns, made poor decisions, had many bad relationships and all together wasted at least fifteen years of his life. Life as a druggie is not glamorous. He feels that he came out better than most of the people that were really into the drug culture.

He has seen society change so much over the decades. He believes we have become more humane, while caring less for others. As we become more successful and acquisitive, we care less for those around us. He believes people do not seem to have any true feelings for other people anymore, or maybe he has just been exposed to some terrible people for many years.

When he walks now, he tries to clear his mind and often has an optimistic thought. He will continue to wear his sunglasses and be proud of an innocent generation that thought that someday they could make a difference. And maybe they did.

The Countess de Lloyd

She told people she was a Countess, and the occasion never arose to question this claim. This is probably because no one believed her in the first place.

Born in 1925, she grew into a beautiful young woman that resembled a contemporary of hers—the film star, Hedy Lamar. She had the same raven black hair and dark eyes. Added to her charm was her French accent.

She lived in Europe during the Second World War.

In 1939 she was 14 when the war began. Her mother always said it was the war that changed her as she had always been a good girl. This disclosure was accompanied with a shake of the head.

In 1945, she met the handsome Kentucky gentleman, who had an uncanny resemblance to the actor Lloyd Nolan. They married. She did not know this was a rebound marriage. The 32-year-old major had married her in what some could call a vindictive act in reaction to a letter he received from his sister. The woman to whom he was engaged was 'running around' with soldiers in their hometown.

Hurt, seeking solace, he married the 19-year-old girl. There was a 13-year difference in their ages. She told him she was 23.

She barely spoke English, but she was assigned to help interrogate a captured German soldier. She was then sent to see the major to deliver the information that was gathered. After meeting, the major asked her to dinner. Within months, they married.

The war was soon over, and she took a long sea voyage to reach him in his U.S. home. It was a small southern town not accustomed to foreigners.

Did she choose de Lloyd because of the major's resemblance to the film stars?

That can be the only explanation.

The marriage was not a happy one and by 1950 she had begun to drink daily. Seeking help, the major sent her to a psychiatrist with whom she had an affair.

The doctor diagnosed her as a paranoid schizophrenic.

Life became increasingly difficult for all that knew her. But how well did anyone know her?

Yes, she called herself The Countess de Lloyd; I called her Mother.

Lasting

Leaving flowers on someone's grave is for the living.
It shows others that a person was cared for, is thought about
and missed. I suppose some believe the dearly departed
know of their visits and are pleased that flowers have been
left on their graves. Mick Jagger sang "Dead Flowers" and
promised, "I won't forget to put roses on your grave."

Where and when did this custom begin? Well, that
information is findable. The practice of leaving flowers at
graves began thousands of years ago when the ancient
Greeks would honor fallen warriors. Their reason for doing
so is beautiful. They believed that if flowers rooted into the
ground, and grew from the gravesite, it was a sign that the
fallen had found peace.

When a long-lasting flower arrangement is placed on
graves, it is an Immortelle.

Immortelle is a flower, Helichchrysum arenarium,
which also makes 'everlasting tea'. As flowers, they retain
their color when dried and are used in arrangements.

Which shall I put on his grave? The chrysanthemum
or carnation will last the longest if that is what I want.

As I research the meaning of certain flowers to leave
on a grave, I am unsure which to choose.

Roses are the most popular flowers to be found in
the cemetery. Each color has its own symbolic
representation. A pink rose for example, is admiration or
joy a red rose passion and a yellow friendship.

As I weigh the decision over a solution occurs to me.
I will leave a bouquet of every color rose possible. It says all;

it is every emotion I felt for him. I feel at peace. As I said, flowers are for the living.

Dead Conversations

What if the dead all congregated and compared notes on their cause of death.

One exclaims, "I had it comin'", another "But I looked both ways."

There are the suicides who honestly felt they had good reason, despite being told it is a permanent solution to a temporary problem.

Women, the victims of an outraged man's fists pummeling them senseless, wail at their misfortunes. The children, in their innocence, are genuinely confused about death and it remains a mystery to them. There is no parent there to explain, so they whimper in despair.

The brave men that fought the many battles and lost their lives feel complete. Their roles in life satisfied. The pilots, soldiers, sailors made the supreme sacrifice and are remembered well. They share their deaths with pride and surprisingly, do not condemn the one's that sent them to war.

There are those that died from a policeman's bullet, and these are often open for debate as to why there was a good reason to shoot them. The unrepentant criminals declare an unjust death while the others know it was murder that took their lives. The executed have their own tales to tell, about hanging or electrocution or even being shot at dawn. They all have their stories.

Death whether justified or not, is the final walk on earth never to experience a good cup of coffee or a tasty meal again.

This congregation with all their narratives, and there are more, all seem to join in the same conclusion...at times it was great to be alive.

Geyser

Big news in the neighborhood. A water main two blocks from our house burst. The excitement among the kids was palpable; everyone wanted to see the spectacle. My cousin and I wanted to as well. After numerous questions, which culminated in extorting a promise not to take off our shoes, we were allowed to go.

There was a crowd gathered and folks were mostly milling about. The water that lapped at our ankles was cold and refreshing this July day. We remained a while, but soon decided it was best to return home.

Completing the first block we stopped to put on our socks and shoes. By the next block we were prepared for the obvious question. We, of course, claimed that we had not removed our shoes and the topic was dropped.

The next day the morning paper had on the front page a picture of us with socks and shoes in hand wading in the water. Despite the fact that the adults found it amusing and we escaped punishment, I learned a valuable lesson.

A Memory

She first met Arthur Birch when she was 13; he was 15. He crashed her girlfriend's slumber party with some of his buddies.

He was brash and had a quick smile. His peroxide blonde hair made him stand out from the other boys.

A few years later he and his family moved around the corner from her. She wanted to date him but was not allowed to, as he was Catholic. This was the high school years.

After graduation, she did not realize that she chose the same university that he had begun to attend the year before. Their paths crossed and he was kind and helpful on that first day of class registration.

That summer they returned to their hometown and dated casually until she learned he was seen out with another girl.

After that there were chance meetings every few years or so. Then, around Christmas one year, they saw one another in a shop. She said, "Give me a call sometime," and he did. She did not receive his call enthusiastically and he suggested she call him next time. She never did.

A few more years passed and once again they saw one another in a home improvement store. This time she agreed to have dinner with him.

Now older and wiser, she asked him why he never married. He paused and replied, "When it came time to marry, I decided why bother."

That was the last time she saw him.

He died peacefully 15 years later; his brother was by his side.

IF

Called the biggest little word in the dictionary, sums this two-letter concept up well. How many times a day is this voiced?

While reading a biographical piece about Janis Joplin, the word kept creeping into the profile. There were so many missed opportunities that could have prevented her death. But why always look back saying 'if only." A plaintive wish which means absolutely nothing in the scheme of things.

Lucinda Williams' song says "If wishes were horses, I'd have a ranch." Again, expressing most likely an impossibility. Imagine the word was banished from our vocabulary. Would we begin saying assuming that, granted that, on condition that, and so on?

So may it remain in the human lexicon, as we will inevitably have reason to use it.

IF the occasion arises.

Prescient

To be told as a child, by an angry adult, "Damn your eyes" were words that came back to her as she was dealing with an eye condition. She was told she would eventually go blind. Was she cursed or did the adult predict her future?

Two weeks before she retired, she was delivered a blow as the doctor diagnosed macular degeneration. Ironically, she was retiring from Recordings for the Blind.

In childhood she pretended to be blind, unfortunately, this portrayal would be at the dinner table. She abandoned this practice after overturning a pitcher of milk. Again, she drew wrath from an adult.

So, in the last 10 years of her life, she will most likely experience the progress of her malady. As she often says, "I hope I die before I go blind." She repeats her words, despite realizing that this is unfair to all those brave, blind individuals that have spent their lives, or most of their lives, in darkness.

She likes to think, on the lighter side, that this condition is a good excuse for having missed sweeping the corners of the kitchen where dust seems to accumulate.

And...Nancy

She had an allergy to lanolin and disliked sunlight. Her tastes ran to tales of Dracula, although later in life she began reading romance novels.

She disliked school and only graduated from high school because her mother promised her a car if she finished that last year.

She spent her days nearly the same. Awaken, drink coffee, read, feed her cats.

Other than that, she did little else.

She sometimes listened to music with headphones and would hum or sing along.

A smile was rare and a laugh even more so. Tears could never be found in her eyes.

She lived her life and died. Few wept or knew of her existence. End of story.

Four Last Things

In his 1522 book, by this title, the phrase "A penny for your thoughts" was 'coined'. Still in use today, the question has survived 500 years.

Now, why am I telling you this? She has been leaving a penny on her father's grave ever since she read that it means the deceased is in the person's thoughts.

The penny keeps disappearing. Once she found it nearby. But where did the other penny go?

She thinks she knows. It is a former lover who, she imagines, takes the penny to confuse her or annoy her. Why else?

If she ever sees him again, she will share her thoughts with him. Until then, the little manufactured mystery remains.

Dead Girls

Hats off to those suicides that had the nerve or were at a point of desperation or had merely had enough. They either slit their wrists or succumb to an overdose of pills. Their life is over, this is the end of their story...usually.

It was a revelation to me to hear about the dead girls. They were mentioned briefly on a radio show. Those girls that long for death. Their days were spent imagining their final breath.

These adolescent girls formed a union trying to hasten their deaths. They swore to help one another when or if necessary. This is the story of four of those girls.

Alvina Hollingsworth, Mary Talbot, Lillian French, and Kate Davis. Each had their own method for their demise.

Alvina was a romantic. She spent her days daydreaming of one love that she held so dear. As fate would have it, her love was rejected, and her heart was broken. This heightened the sense of urgency for this 17-year-old girl. She wanted to join the dead, many of whom she believed had also experienced broken hearts. She found her father's pistol, placed it against her heart and pulled the trigger. It was the end of her pain. It is rare for a female to choose this method. But for her it was quick and final.

Mary was a quiet, pensive girl. At 16 she knew she no longer wished to live. Her plan was simple, she was a poor sleeper and against the better judgement of her parents, they had her prescriptions filled for a sleep medication.

Mary took the meds occasionally, but these pills were her way out. She surreptitiously hoarded the pills for months, always asking for a monthly refill to which her parents complied. When Mary felt she had stockpiled enough she bid her parents good night lovingly and headed for bed. Once there and alone, she took nearly one hundred sleeping pills. Her parents found her the following morning, dead with a smile on her face.

Now this is the case of Lillian French. Her method was as drastic as Alvina's. Lillian cut her wrists with a razor blade she removed from her mother's razor. She cut the tips of her fingers terribly trying to remove the slender razor. She too was 17 and was meticulously tidy, so her method of ending her life was surprising. She settled herself in the bathtub to avoid a mess and applied the razor to the wrists of both arms. She bled out and died peacefully.

And finally, there is Kate Davis. At 16, she was a member of the high school swimming team, but she found little pleasure in competing. Kate loved the water and would often sink to the bottom of the pool trying to force herself to stay under the water. Following an impulse, she drove to the river that separated her state from another.

Approaching the bridge, she threw herself into the turbulent water below. She felt nothing when she hit the water and sank, drowning in her descent.

This is the story of the four girls, four dead girls, that knew what they wanted and went for it.

The Stolen Cane with Various Alternatives

Left in an unlocked car lay the beautifully carved wooden cane. It was propped against the back seat. The cane went missing. A thief quickly opened the door, grabbed the cane, and made off with it. Days passed, and the owner continued to be dismayed by the theft of the cane, as it had been made by someone dear.

Then one day, not too long after, the cane appeared at the back door. A mystery indeed. There were several possible reasons for its return.

One may suspect remorse, thought by the good at heart. Or possibly a young one, a neighborhood scamp, returned home with it only to confess his thievery to a questioning mother. Perhaps, thought by the realist.

Maybe the cane theft was spotted by a passing neighbor and a chase ensued. Finally in fright as the pursuer was gaining on him, the cane was tossed aside.

The victor, being a humble soul, wanted no thanks and certainly did not want to relate the event to anyone. He left the stolen cane at the back door. One attracted to heroism and adventure may think that.

Then there could have been the neighbor who subtly says, "Lock your car door."

Again, a thought that could be shared by the good at heart.

This can only close with who knows?

73

The "Farmer"

We were seating ourselves in the Mojito bar and restaurant in Miami, when a bearded young man said, beer in hand, "This place is a "rip off."" He was right.

Next, he said that he was going to sit down and talk to us.

His red beard was long and accented the poor condition of his teeth. With his face pressed towards mine, he said his girlfriend was "over there." It was obvious that he did not heed the sign posted on the wall asking people to drink responsibly and that it could cause the airline to refuse to let them board the plane.

Our conversation began. I asked his occupation and he replied, "I'm a cook."

My puzzled look produced the words "I am a chef. But I used to be a farmer." He says these words in the well-known hand gesture to indicate quotes.

He told us he lived in Maine for 20 years. They were in Miami to take the second part of their journey home. They had been on a cruise to the Caribbean.

As our orders of rice bowls arrived, he said he better check on his girlfriend.

We turned to bid him farewell, and he had already been swallowed up by the airport crowd.

My Enemy the Anemone?

When he told her their relationship was like the sea anemone and the clown fish, she immediately remarked, "With you as the clown fish?"

"Of course," he retorted.

Knowing nothing of the relationship between these two aquatic organisms, she was dismayed when her sister told her the sea anemone kills clown fish. She searched for clues to his remark.

When he asked her if she loved him sometimes, and tolerated him at other times, she was non-plussed and replied, "I tolerate you because I love you."

Which was ridiculous since she barely knew him.

Research reveals the symbiotic relationship between an anemone and a clown fish. It is a classic example of two organisms benefiting the other. The anemone provides the clown fish with protection and shelter, while the clown fish provides the anemone nutrients in the form of waste, while also scaring off predator fish.

With this newly gained knowledge she understood his statement better. Now she demands to herself, "Where do we go from here?"

Contents Under Pressure

We all have to blow off steam. We need to release that pent up valve that accumulates pressure as tensions within the day seem to mount and have to find a way of releasing themselves. My release is writing.

I hope to express fear, sadness, and elation. Stress in today's busy world is as much a part of everyday life as their morning cup of coffee or the daily paper.

I am sure I am not telling anyone something that they do not already know and hey, who wants to read about stress anyway? We know what it is, and we all have our own way of dealing with it.

Fear too has become a part of daily life. We fear for ourselves, we fear for our children, the country, warring nations. The list could go on ad infinitum.

Fears are like the rain. We can try to avoid it, we can try to protect ourselves from it but it is relentless, as there is nothing we can do to stop it.

Sadness, unlike depression, is not always a bad emotion. Being sad can tell a person that they are human and alive, much like being happy. Sadness can show depth of character, a different level of perceiving the world. Sadness like joy can be caused by events or memories. It can overtake you in a second and change your day or your hour or your life.

Elation is the most rare and difficult to discuss. Yet to be elated can result from something as simple as completing a crossword puzzle accurately. This you may say would merely be satisfaction, but some could actually feel elation from such an accomplishment. I suppose it would depend on how often a person works a crossword puzzle.

So here it is, my reasons for writing and some of my topics. I hope I will find pleasure from this writing and from the release of stress and the creativity that can be forthcoming.

Mon Oncle

He died at 47 from emphysema. He was a three pack a day smoker from the age of 16. Raised by a seemingly single mother, his father had a nebulous background. The mother ended up in Berea, California with yet another husband, and this one struck oil in his front yard.

The last years of my uncle's life were difficult for everyone. His devoted wife, my dad's sister, cared for him in their home after his tracheotomy. He required daily oxygen treatments. Once, during the night, he stopped breathing, and she carried the 6-foot oxygen tank over to his bedside to revive him.

The night he died, he gently squeezed her hand, held it, and drifted away.

Greer

Now whenever I drink a beer,
I am always reminded of that girl Greer.
In my heart she was held so dear,
Even now as the police draw near,
She said she'd always love me,
And would never go away.
But I held my breath and waited,
And knew she would someday.
When she came to me with a laugh and a start,
She slowly
Methodically
Broke my heart.
She taunted and teased and laughed at me,
I was driven to madness, can't you see?
And around her throat I placed my hands,
And with my fingers I formed a band.
I squeezed and waited 'til her face turned blue,
I watched the realization as she finally knew.
To me she had told her final lie,
And now, by my hands she was going to die.
I think of this and await the blue-clad mister,
How was I to know that Greer was his sister?

Anything But Me[*]

I wish I was a fluffy cloud,
Anything but me.
A blade of grass,
A pane of glass,
Anything but me.
No! Is what they say,
Any time I want to play.
Big brothers sure can be a bore,
And big sisters even more.
No one wants to play with me,
And I'm lonely can't you see.

[*] This was written for a girl child who is now an actress living in New York.

The 25 Steps

Have you heard the expression "if walls could talk?"

I am sure you have, but have you ever wondered if stairs could speak? Well, yes, they can. I know because they have spoken to me. I have a talent for speaking with the dead.

I first saw the stairs while attending a promotional event in an old building on Market Street. The building was constructed around 1850 and has hosted many visitors since then. As I approached the stairs, I was struck by the impressions accosting me. They were vying for my attention. They merely wanted to tell their stories.

As my foot rests on the top step, a male voice speaks out to me. He says his name is Preston Smith. Then he says 1800 to 1856 telling me what are apparently his birth and death dates. He was a successful doctor in New York City and married a rich widow ten years his senior. He studied in his hometown then moved to New York to further his career.

Upon his death, he was returned to his hometown and laid to rest in the beautiful cemetery that he chose to be his final destination.

Suddenly a dulcet tone from the second step interrupts his dialogue, "Preston, dear, I am right behind you." By way of introduction she says her name, "Thomasina".

She does not give the birth or death date and as if by apology she tells me demurely that she has been married before. Her first husband was extremely wealthy, as he owned an oil enterprise. She was widowed only one year after their marriage. He died in a carriage accident in the streets of New York City. He left her well-off and when she met Preston, she knew she wanted to spend the rest of her life with him. She proposed and they never looked back as they traveled from New York City to Charlestown, South Carolina to stay in their summer home. She pouts that she had been accused of being untruthful about her age but as she says it is every woman's prerogative.

Unsure what or who my next step would summon, I stepped deliberately on the third step reaching toward the foyer below. I was amused by the introduction to the next spirit.

Bland Ballard spoke in his onomatopoeic voice that 1820 to1870 was his life span. He wistfully said he had been a mediocre politician that tried to institute change for the better but was thwarted by those that chose currency over humanity. I made a mental note that not one has told me the manner of their death only their life which I find consoling.

Upon reaching the fourth stair step Henry Pride 1825 to 1875 adds forwardly, "I was a lawyer, editor, historian and was a partner of Bland Ballard. I would like to express my respect for Bland and I hope he hears every word."

These voices have revealed a response to a question that I have often asked myself. Do the spirits know one another and can they communicate with one another? It is apparent they can.

Anxious in my descent to reach the fifth step I then slowly, reticently lower my right foot then my left foot. As my foot touches the step a low moan can be heard. It is a woman's mournful lament.

Hattie Wilson cried, "1850 to 1914."

Hattie reveals she was a contemporary of Carrie Nation, a radical member of the temperance movement. She went right along with the axe-wielding, bottle smashing temperance leader. Hattie says she decided to go one further and take an alcoholic drink in order to better condemn the beverage. From that first sip, she became dependent on alcohol and the cause for her was permanently lost.

After hearing this tale of woe, I was hoping the sixth step would be a bit more uplifting and so it came to be.

Sally Callahan, 1823 to 1907, spoke out and identified herself as a nurse during the war between the states. She was 37 at the time, and although for the South, she nursed many a Union soldier. The compassion in her voice was all I needed to erase the haunting voice of the previous spirit.

As seven rhymes with heaven, I hoped for something, anything as I was greeted with silence treading upon the seventh step. Finally, a deep baritone spoke slowly in his introduction. Clark Prather said 1846 to 1899 in his solemn, ghostly voice. He reveals he is a spokesman for heaven as a devout minister that, he claims, saved many a soul with his impassioned sermons. Feeling rewarded and myself gifted I nearly pounce upon the eighth step.

Much to my satisfaction another woman's voice wafts towards me from the number eight.

Edith George declares 1843 to 1890. Edith tells me she was a librarian inside the Central Market building, the first library in her state in 1872. It is enough of a statement to define her and her gratifying life.

Matthew Gordon spoke up as I tread upon the ninth step while very slowly moving downward.

I am deliberately descending slowly so as not to discourage my next revelation from the departed.

Matthew proceeds to say 1790 to 1875.

He was a builder responsible for much of the construction in a budding metropolis begun in 1820. He is quick to say he was successful in business but unlucky in love. With this, he will reveal no more about himself.

The tenth step consumed my interest as Spencer Whiteman 1819 to1893 made himself known. He divulged his Dublin birthplace as well as relating his success as a trained architect focusing on the Italian Renaissance. Many buildings reflect his work and his influence.

Next, I tread upon the eleventh step of this fascinating and enlightening brick building. Beforehand, I gave little thought to the material with which the building was constructed. As I indulge in this thought I wonder if each brick, as each step, has a spirit lingering within wishing to share their life.

A lyrical voice greeted me as I stepped upon the twelfth step. This voice was cultured with a slight accent.

"Lydia Anderson." she says adding, "1890 to 1942".

She continues, "I began to sing at the age of 3 or so I am told. I studied abroad and lived there for some time. Upon my return I was entertained in some of the best homes. Many sought status by welcoming an opera singer into their midst. I was 24 when the war started and I did special performances to entertain the troops. I do hope I am remembered well.

The landing was, I considered, my thirteenth step and I was rewarded by the next spirit, Walter Washington, who announced his presence with,

"1819 to 1892, poet laureate. I visited many towns as I traveled and lectured."

Walter confides that his work was controversial yet there is a certain amount of pride in his disclosure.

Descending from the landing, I gazed at the remaining twelve steps and gingerly stepped upon the fourteenth step or the first step depending upon your point of view. Suddenly an anguished voice assailed my senses with its wail.

Silas Newman identified himself with 1823 to 1907. He says his profession as a pharmacist was a disaster. There was a patient seeking relief from a toothache.

He continues with "the patient was allergic to morphine; it restricted his breathing and he suffocated."

The pharmacist did not question any allergies when he filled the prescription, he bitterly says the doctor should have been to blame but with his influence in the community, "I was condemned and took to drink."

By the fifteenth step I was prepared for anything as Foster Douglas exclaimed his name along with 1821 to 1902. Foster says he was a gambler and a damn good one. He was lucky at cards, dice, roulette. He spent many years in New Orleans on riverboats. "To me," he says, "life is meant to be a risk, a gamble and you have got to gamble if you want to win."

The next step, number sixteen, brought forth Bailey St. John, who said forcefully, "1864 until 1936." He prides himself as having been a successful Chief of Police for the L & N railroad. He adds that he captured many a train robber, swindler, anyone that dared to break the law while he was in charge. He also says that his adventures are chronicled in magazine publications by the railroad.

Astounded by the array of spirits that have visited this building and left their stories behind, I moved to the seventeenth step expectantly.

Harris Matthews first says his occupation, artist, then 1814 to1881. Harris divulged that he was a favored student of Gilbert Stuart who was considered America's foremost portraitist. Harris' work, he says, includes a portrait of Henry Clay. He says he enjoyed his life's work.

The eighteenth step was a surprise from the moment that Harriet Collins introduced herself mysteriously as a woman magician and utters, "1900 to 1972." I decided against questioning why she arrived on the scene so much later than the other souls and truthfully, she may not know.

She explains that she traveled extensively, making appearances at county and state fairs. She says her magic was more than smoke and mirrors.

Robert Paul describes himself as a Renaissance man. This nineteenth step brings forth a concert artist that says 1898 to 1976 in his rich bass baritone voice. He imparts this information with his disclosure that he was a political activist and a professional football player. He must truly have been a man of action.

When I reached the twentieth step, Hallie Benedict said 1864 to 1928. She proudly shares that she was a confectioner and caterer. She claims her business was an institution on Fourth Street. Upon hearing this I realize I know of her culinary creation and routinely buy it at the market.

The twenty-first step launches me closer to the present again with a woman sculptor. She says, "1870 to 1934, my name is Yolanda Enid."

I enjoy that she speaks of herself in the present. She thinks of the time she spent in France apprenticing in the workshop of Rodin. Her statues can be seen scattered about the city.

With the twenty-second step Benjamin Taylor regales me, opening with 1907 to 1982. He also informs me that he was a professor at the state university and was renowned for his lectures.

Thomas Stoddard was to be found lounging at twenty-three. He said in his southern accent, "1823 to 1913, ma'am." Thomas was a confederate soldier and a lawyer.

He stayed in his hometown, he shared he never wanted to go anywhere else.

As I place my foot on the twenty-fourth step, I realize I have only one last step to encounter. That is when the high-pitched woman's voice says, "Jennie Davis. 1938 to 1990." She was the widow of a Dr. Davis and is closer than anyone to my time. She reveals that she was only known as the wife of the successful heart surgeon.

I had finally reached the twenty-fifth and final step of this long stairway which was divided by the landing. I marveled that the time spent descending the stairs was very brief for all the spirits I encountered. Bendigo Combs spoke up from this final step, saying 1830 to1900. He was a carpenter that worked in the building, which included the construction of the stairs. He enjoyed his work and is delighted that the building has survived urban renewal. When I questioned how he knew about urban renewal he responded oh we know many things. He says the stairs are just as sturdy as when they were built. His voice fades as I reach the floor and walk away turning to gaze up at the stairway.

I did not question why the phantoms all rose out of the wooden steps to share what, to them, was a brief life in which they all entered the building and climbed the stairs.

Why there? Why them? There is no definitive answer to that.

When I exited the building and turned down the sidewalk from the building facade I heard, "Hello?"

Sondra

We knew her, not well, just as a fellow co-worker. Her sense of humor was amusing only to herself. She wanted to be friends but I, like others, was reluctant due to her abrasive personality. She was obviously intelligent, but was rarely warm or caring.

Sondra had two sons, was divorced and bitter. We couldn't help but think at the end her ex probably detested her. Some of the other colleagues in the department chose to ridicule her due to her unusual quirks and daily complaints. One such worker said if a large bag of money was placed on her desk, she would complain that the bag was too heavy and that she would prefer smaller bills.

Years passed and we both stayed with the job, never seeking other employment. I liked the research position as apparently so did she. I concluded that she enjoyed correcting narrators on their pronunciations and that there were not too many people to encounter, which would have been a plus for her.

Often, we would take a walk during lunch break accompanied by another member of the research team. At one time the three of us would meet up on a weekend evening to prepare a sumptuous meal. The disturbing part of this activity was the huge amount of gin she consumed. Finally, as a result, we discontinued our culinary pursuits.

More years passed, and I retired from the company, as she was 5 years younger, she had to wait to leave the profession. In the presence of the other worker who was male, she was very confrontational with me. So, when she asked me to come to walk with her, with or without him, I made excuses. Finally, we lost touch.

Roughly three years passed, and our male chum said he had seen her, they walked, but she was unable to go far, she sat on some church steps, and it was a struggle for him to get her to her feet again. He finally succeeded and he brought his car to retrieve her and return her to her small apartment. After that, there was no word from her.

A month later he called me; he was worried about her. He had called her sons as both had left the area, one living abroad, the other across the country. The ex-husband was contacted, and he sent the police to her residence.

They had to break down the door in order to get to her. There they found her, quite dead, with liquor bottles strewn about the room.

May she rest in peace, a peace she never knew in life.

The Occupant

As the landlord of a small two-bedroom house, she placed an ad on a local rental website. The house was located three houses from the proprietor and was empty as the previous renter had been evicted.

One of the first applicants was a young, single mother. The application revealed she was an event planner for a large hotel chain. Her son was four. The information and references checked out and a one-year lease was signed. The rent was reasonable at $750 per month, and woman and boy promptly moved in.

At year's end the tenant expressed interest in buying the house and was sorely disappointed that the house was not for sale. The renter was also disappointed that the landlord was doing well and in fine health. She did remain another year with no signing of another lease. The rent stayed the same.

They were entering the third year of rental when the owner began noticing a different, older car, parked in the driveway. When the tenant was questioned, she said her sister was now living there as well. Apparently, the sister was having some financial difficulties. This did not pose a problem, so nothing further was said.

Two more years passed and there was never an increase in rent as was promised. Then the owner began noticing different cars parked in the driveway. So, one evening, with a friend, she knocked on the door of the rental. There was no answer. She entered the house and inside she found a young man and an elderly woman.

When questioned about who they were the man said "I am her brother." The woman was the mother. This did not ring true as the tenant had no brother. The landlord decided not to question the two further and left. That began a quest to find out the truth.

In checking a site on Willow, the proprietor discovered that her "tenant" was running an ad to rent out the house for $950. She claimed to be the property manager. Next, the owner questioned one of the neighbors, who knew something about the tenant. It was disclosed that the father of the tenant's child said the mother was no good and could become violent.

The plan of action was to email the "tenant" with Willow rental in the subject line. With that, the owner asked who was living in her house and was again told it was her sister, who was now in a financial position to rent the house alone. The next attempt to clear up the matter occurred when a letter was placed in the rental house's mailbox demanding that the house be vacated immediately or the police would be called. Within an hour a tearful woman appeared at the door. She was not the tenant's sister but a friend and thought the tenant owned the house. The inhabitant tried to reach the tenant but got no response.

They had known one another for years. Naturally, her reaction was hurt and anger.

The landlord accepted her pleas to be allowed to stay. References were checked and she stayed. Three more years have passed, and all has gone smoothly. The two friends have never spoken again.

The Fifty-Year Stalker

Yes, that is right, fifty-years. She didn't know his name but knew his face, she remembered him from all those years ago. Their paths crossed less than occasionally, but they never exchanged words other than the first time they met.

It was in a local pub frequented by many people of approximately the same age. She remembers standing at the bar engaging in disinterested conversation with him. She told him she was married but that did not dissuade him, then another fellow entered by the side door. That got her attention. Upon telling the soon to be stalker her husband's name, he said, "Oh, not that New Jersey faggot."

Knowing her mate wasn't from New Jersey, nor gay, she gave him no other thought as she walked away in order to speak with the friend that entered the room.

During the following years she only saw him three times, once at a convenience store, and twice at the grocery store. While shopping, they made eye contact. She had tucked her head in thought, but it had nothing to do with him. She did notice a look of triumph in his face as he realized she recognized him from years before. The other time there was no eye contact, but she noticed he looked embarrassed as he was accompanied by his, what she thought, two children.

The last time she saw him was at the 7-11, mentioned earlier. As she exited the store, she heard him say to the clerk, "Let me tell you something about her!"

Afterwards, the clerks at the store were not so friendly as before.

Now fast-forward thirty years and the arrival of social media. This stalker was able to determine her name and share her photo with anyone that cared to look before she changed to friends only status. She was so short-sighted regarding this communication phenomenon that has caused more problems than being able to provide useful information.

The stalker was observing posts between her and an old friend of hers, Thomas. She regrets sending the message which indicated when and where she would be walking. And it happened, Thomas showed up there. They had a history and she felt she needed to do the right thing.

They did not speak the first time because she didn't recognize him then she regrets she wrote to ask if that was indeed him that she saw at her walking place. Unfortunately, Thomas was there a second time. She was taken aback but professed to be happy to see him and after 3 hours of chatting she was happy to have seen him again.

The stalker was there that day and misunderstood a reply to her query to Thomas who loudly exclaimed, "I don't care". The stalker thought that it was meant about him.

Since then, the stalker has become a talker. She can no longer go to her favorite walking spot because of stares and comments. Four years have passed, and she found other places to walk and other groceries to go to. And to this day, she has never known his name.

How to Kill Your Publisher

How many writers have had that inclination? Their cries, their pleas, fall upon deaf ears or could I say deaf years.   Deadlines, expectations, yet also can be found, which is difficult to admit, good ideas and inspiration.

In response to a demand, can a writer demand more time?   One must let the creative juices flow. And to think, just think of something that can be written, or should be written.

The writer is an open book, and the publisher is illiterate.   Do they not understand the writing process? One cannot write on command. Sure, there are some topics percolating in the brain.   Those ideas accumulate and are put on paper or screen when the time is right.   It can be compared in a sense to a painter that knows when to stop on a painting, the writer knows when to begin.

Now the project found in the title can be resolved or completed by the publisher dying at the hands of the writer. The numerous articles, stories, ideas, changes, questions can bombard the publisher, and this is a "possible" manner of disposing of the adversary.

Now, just for interest in this subject what is the point of view of the publisher?   Yes, yes, aside from money.   Do they claim to be in it for the art, to promote the works and ideas of authors?   In today's world much is done with self- publishing which must include editing and proofing.   So,indeed there can be understanding of a publisher's motivations.

That is the Hand I was Dealt

Really?
She says she has always had a plan going through life.
Hmm
Ignorance is bliss would be my credo, if I didn't
already know.
Truth
He was convenient for me. I had someone, yet I
didn't. We shared no geographical space—and he traveled
to distant lands.
Sadly said
When informed that someone had commented that
they had always considered her smart, she replied I have
never been accused of that!!
Yes
People can have a higher purpose—and have no faith
in a superior being.
Our Song
Only had one with anyone, it was "Excitable Boy" by
Warren Zevon.
Memory
Leaving a matchbox cover from a Louisville pub on
a wall in Amsterdam.
Margaret's Wisdom
Be kind to those that are unkind to you, it hurts
them worse.
And...
Where does the spirit go?
Baked

I use the olfactory process when baking, if you can smell it, it is done.

Spectacles

I just read that Elton John damaged his eyes by wearing Buddy Holly's glasses constantly.

No One Knows

It is called speculation when you think you know what another person is thinking.

Love the term

BoBo is a French term for someone that is Bohemian and Bourgeoisie.

In Beatnik terms

It was a real drag.

Easter

It is the first Sunday after the first full moon that occurs on or after the Spring equinox...how pagan.

Hello Winter Moon

Nothing quite so magical as a full moon in January.

Cracker Barrel

Always uncomfortable there as the old photos remind me of the ones I have of relatives on my walls at home.

She never knew

What her visit to the hospital meant.

Music

My refuge as I don't like being alone with my thoughts.

Us

I like to think we are not conventional people.

A Reason Explained

She is evil and just can't help it.

The Hardware Store

Always remember going there with my dad, the smells, the odd assortment of gadgets...nostalgia at its best.

Chocolate

I am the bittersweet variety.

Me

Don't be self-conscious. People don't pay that much attention.

Bashful Pride.

Is that an oxymoron?

Midnight

The adopted black cat, 6 years of age, I love his breed.

Realization

I don't want to jump through a lot of hoops.

Sometimes

I just want to be an apple and say, "Bite me."

Life

I had no instructions.

Memorable People

From a fellow airline passenger "how did you get that knot on your head?"

Me

Living in a country where I don't understand the language is almost as good as being deaf.

Another Thought

People should be held accountable for what they say.

Him

He wants a place in my head no matter how he gets it.

Me

No one brings me down quite as much as I do.

Who Could Write my Life?

Tennessee Williams

Meditation and Tofu

I like the idea but not the experience.

Domestic

I love the sound of my washing machine.

Reality

We all have an expiration date.

Look closely

Without proper punctuation, a sentence looks undressed, disheveled.

Urge

To yell "We're all gonna die" as a plane begins to lift off.

Sound Imagery

The rustling sounds of leaves in trees, in the fall.

Reality

I heal, you heal, we all heal. It is all part of the process.

A Question

Music has meant everything to me.

How Often

Do you think of me?

Say Nothing

Grand-mere, I never do that, j'ai la cœur ouvert.

It is Difficult

Paranoia and perspicacity are two traits that are a double-edged sword.

Oh!!

She loves the handprints on the glass door. She cherishes each moment.

Hmm

The beauty in sending cards rather than texts, no one know what time you wrote it.

Fogerty

Memories and Elephants

Peeling Apples

Good time for reflexion.